# HORRID HENRY
# Wakes the Dead

Francesca Simon spent her childhood on the beach
in California, and then went to Yale and Oxford
Universities to study medieval history and literature.
She now lives in London with her family. She has
written over 50 books and won the Children's Book
of the Year in 2008 at the Galaxy British Book Awards
for *Horrid Henry and the Abominable Snowman*.

# HORRiD HENRY
# Wakes the Dead

Francesca Simon
*Illustrated by* Tony Ross

Orion
Children's Books

ORION CHILDREN'S BOOKS

First published in Great Britain in 2009 by Orion Children's Books
This edition published in 2016 by Hodder and Stoughton

9

Text copyright © Francesca Simon, 2009
Illustrations copyright © Tony Ross, 2009

The moral rights of the author and illustrator have been asserted.

A CIP catalogue record for this book
is available from the British Library.

ISBN 978 1 4072 3036 8

Printed and bound in Great Britain
by Clays Ltd, St Ives plc

The paper and board used in this book are
made from wood from responsible sources.

Orion Children's Books
An imprint of
Hachette Children's Group
Part of Hodder and Stoughton
Carmelite House
50 Victoria Embankment
London EC4Y 0DZ

An Hachette UK Company
www.hachette.co.uk

www.hachettechildrens.co.uk
www.horridhenry.co.uk

*For Steven Butler*
*the original Horrid Henry*

# CONTENTS

......................................................

# HORRID HENRY AND THE TV REMOTE

Horrid Henry pushed through the front door. Perfect Peter squeezed past him and ran inside.

'Hey!' screamed Horrid Henry, dashing after him. 'Get back here, worm.'

'Noooo!' squealed Perfect Peter, running as fast as his little legs would carry him.

Henry grabbed Peter's shirt, then hurtled past him into the sitting room. Yippee! He was going to get the comfy black chair first. Almost there, almost there, almost . . . and then Horrid Henry skidded on a sock and slipped. Peter pounded past and dived onto the comfy black chair. Panting and gasping, he snatched the remote control. Click!

'All together now! Who's a silly Billy?' trilled the world's most annoying goat.

'Billy!' sang out Perfect Peter.

NOOOOOOOOOOOOO!

It had happened again. Just as Henry was looking forward to resting his weary bones on the comfy black chair after another long, hard, terrible day at school and watching *Rapper Zapper* and *Knight Fight*, Peter had somehow managed to nab the chair first. It was so unfair.

The rule in Henry's house was that whoever was sitting in the comfy black chair decided what to watch on TV. And there was Peter, smiling and singing along

with Silly Billy, the revolting singing
goat who thought he was a clown.

Henry's parents were so mean and
horrible, they only had one teeny tiny
telly in the whole,
entire house. It was
so minuscule
Henry practically
had to watch it
using a
magnifying glass.
And so old you
practically had to kick it

to turn it on. Everyone else he knew
had loads of TVs. Rude Ralph had five
ginormous ones all to himself. At least,
that's what Ralph said.

All too often there were at least two
great programmes on at the same time.
How was Henry supposed to choose
between *Mutant Max* and *Terminator
Gladiator*? If only he could watch two
TVs simultaneously, wouldn't life be
wonderful?

Even worse, Mum, Dad, and Peter had
their own smelly programmes *they*
wanted to watch. And not great
programmes like *Hog House* and *Gross
Out*. Oh no. Mum and Dad liked
watching . . . news. Documentaries.
Opera. Perfect Peter liked nature
programmes. And revolting baby
programmes like *Daffy and her Dancing
Daisies*. Uggghh! How did he end up in

this family? When would his real parents, the King and Queen, come and fetch him and take him to the palace where he could watch whatever he wanted all day?

When he grew up and became King Henry the Horrible, he'd have three TVs in every room, including the bathrooms.

But until that happy day, he was stuck at home slugging it out with Peter. He *could* spend the afternoon watching *Silly Billy*, *Cooking Cuties*, and *Sammy the Snail*. Or . . .

Horrid Henry pounced and snatched the remote. CLICK!

'. . . and the black knight lowers his visor . . .'

'Give it to me,' shrieked Peter.

'No,' said Henry.

'But I've got the chair,' wailed Peter.

'So?' said Henry, waving the clicker at him. 'If you want the remote you'll have to come and get it.'

Peter hesitated. Henry dangled the remote just out of reach.

Perfect Peter slipped off the comfy black chair and grabbed for the remote. Horrid Henry ducked, swerved and jumped onto the empty chair.

'. . . And the knights are advancing towards one another, lances poised . . .'

'MUUUUMMMM!' squealed Peter. 'Henry snatched the remote!'

'Did not!'

'Did too.'

'Did not, wibble pants.'

'Don't call me wibble pants,' cried Peter.

'Okay, pongy poo poo,' said Henry.

'Don't call me pongy poo poo,' shrieked Peter.

'Okay, wibble bibble,' said Horrid Henry.

'MUUUUUMMM!' wailed Peter. 'Henry's calling me names!'

'Henry! Stop being horrid,' shouted Mum.

'I'm just trying to watch TV in peace!' screamed Henry. 'Peter's annoying me.'

'Henry's annoying *me*,' whined Peter. 'He pushed me off the chair.'

'Liar,' said Henry. 'You fell off.'

'MUUUUMMMMMM!' screamed Peter.

Mum ran in, and grabbed the remote. Click! The screen went black.

'I've had it with you boys fighting over the TV,' shouted Mum. 'No TV for the rest of the day.'

What?

Huh?

'But . . . but . . .' said Perfect Peter.

'But . . . but . . .' said Horrid Henry.

'No buts,' said Mum.

'It's not fair!' wailed Henry and Peter.

Horrid Henry paced up and down his room, whacking his teddy, Mr Kill, on the bedpost every time he walked past.

WHACK!

WHACK!

WHACK!

He had to find a way to make sure he watched the programmes *he* wanted to watch. He just had to. He'd have to get up at the crack of dawn. There was no other way.

Unless . . .

Unless . . .

And then Horrid Henry had a brilliant, spectacular idea. What an idiot he'd been. All those months he'd missed his fantastic shows . . . Well, never ever again.

Sneak.

    Sneak.

        Sneak.

It was the middle of the night. Horrid Henry crept down the stairs as quietly as he could and tiptoed into the sitting room, shutting the door behind him. There was the TV, grumbling in the corner. 'Why is no one watching me?' moaned the telly. 'C'mon, Henry.'

But for once Henry didn't listen. He had something much more important to do.

He crept to the comfy black chair and fumbled in the dark. Now, where was the remote? Aha! There it was. As usual, it had fallen between the seat cushion and the armrest. Henry grabbed it. Quick as a flash, he switched the TV over to the channel for *Rapper Zapper*, *Talent Tigers* and *Hog House*. Then he tiptoed to the toy cupboard and hid the

remote control deep inside a bucket of
multi-coloured bricks that no
one had played with for
years.

Tee hee, thought
Horrid Henry.

Why should he
have to get up to grab
the comfy black chair
hours before his programmes started
when he could have a lovely lie-in,
saunter downstairs whenever he felt like
it, and be master of the TV? Whoever
was sitting in the chair could be in
charge of the telly all they wanted. But
without the TV remote, no one would
be watching anything.

Perfect Peter stretched out on the comfy
black chair. Hurrah. Serve Henry right
for being so mean to him. Peter had got

downstairs first. Now he could watch what *he* wanted all morning.

Peter reached for the remote control. It wasn't on the armrest. It wasn't on the headrest. Had it slipped between the armrest and the cushion? No. He felt round the back. No. He looked under the chair. Nothing. He looked behind the chair. Where was it?

Horrid Henry strolled into the sitting room. Peter clutched tightly onto the armrests in case Henry tried to push him off.

'I got the comfy black chair first,' said Peter.

'Okay,' said Horrid Henry, sitting down on the sofa. 'So let's watch something.'

Peter looked at Henry suspiciously.

'Where's the remote?' said Peter.

'I dunno,' said Horrid Henry. 'Where did you put it?'

'I didn't put it anywhere,' said Peter.

'You had it last,' said Henry.

'No I didn't,' said Peter.

'Did,' said Henry.

'Didn't,' said Peter.

Perfect Peter sat on the comfy black chair. Horrid Henry sat on the sofa.

'Have you seen it anywhere?' said Peter.

'No,' said Henry. 'You'll just have to look for it, won't you?'

Peter eyed Henry warily.

'I'm waiting,' said Horrid Henry.

Perfect Peter didn't know what to do. If he got up from the chair to look for the remote Henry would jump into it and there was no way Henry would decide to watch *Cooking Cuties*, even though today they were showing how to make your own muesli.

On the other hand, there wasn't much point sitting in the chair if he didn't have the remote.

Henry sat.

Peter sat.

'You know, Peter, you can turn on the TV without the remote,' said Henry casually.

Peter brightened. 'You can?'

'Sure," said Henry. 'You just press that big black button on the left."

Peter stared suspiciously at the button.

Henry must think he was an idiot. He could see Henry's plan from miles away. The moment Peter left the comfy black chair Henry would jump on it.

'You press it,' said Peter.

'Okay,' said Henry agreeably. He sauntered to the telly and pressed the 'on' button.

BOOM! CRASH! WALLOP!

'Des-troy! Des-troy!' bellowed Mutant Max.

'Go Mutants!' shouted Horrid Henry, bouncing up and down.

Perfect Peter sat frozen in the chair.

'But I want to watch *Sing-along with Susie!*' wailed Peter. 'She's teaching a song about raindrops and roses.'

'So find the remote,' said Horrid Henry.

'I can't,' said Peter.

'Tough,' said Horrid Henry. 'Pulverize! Destroy! Destroy!'

Tee hee.


What a fantastic day, sighed Horrid Henry happily. He'd watched every single one of *his* best programmes and Peter hadn't watched a single one of *his*. And now *Hog House* was on. Could life get any better?

Dad staggered into the sitting room. 'Ahh, a little relaxation in front of the telly,' sighed Dad. 'Henry, turn off that horrible programme. I want to watch the news.'

'Shhh!' said Horrid Henry. How dare Dad interrupt him?

'Henry . . .' said Dad.

'I can't,' said Horrid Henry. 'No remote.'

'What do you mean, no remote?' said Dad.

'It's gone,' said Henry.

'What do you mean, gone?' said Mum.

'Henry lost it,' said Peter.

'Didn't,' snapped Henry.

'Did,' said Peter.

'DIDN'T!' bellowed Henry. 'Now be quiet, I'm trying to watch.'

Mum marched over to the telly and switched it off.

'The TV stays off until the remote is found,' said Mum.

'But I didn't lose it!' wailed Peter.

'Neither did I,' said Horrid Henry. This wasn't a lie, as he *hadn't* lost it.

Rats. Maybe it was time for the TV remote to make a miraculous return . . .

Sneak.

Sneak.

Sneak.

Mum and Dad were in the kitchen. Perfect Peter was practising his cello.

Horrid Henry crept to the toy cupboard and opened it.

The bucket of bricks had gone.

Huh?

Henry searched frantically in the cupboard, hurling out jigsaw puzzles, board games, and half-empty paint bottles. The bricks were definitely gone.

Yikes. Horrid Henry felt a chill down his spine. He was dead. He was doomed.

Unless Mum had moved the bricks

somewhere. Of course. Phew. He wasn't
dead yet.

Mum walked into the sitting room.

'Mum,' said Henry casually, 'I wanted
to build a castle with those old bricks
but when I went to get them from the
cupboard they'd gone.'

Mum stared at him. 'You haven't played
with those bricks in years, Henry. I had a
good clear out of all the baby toys today
and gave them to the charity shop.'

Charity shop? Charity shop? That
meant the remote was gone for good.

He would be in trouble. Big big trouble.
He was doomed . . . NOT!

Without the clicker, the TV would be
useless. Mum and Dad would *have* to
buy a new one. Yes! A bigger, better
fantastic one with twenty-five surround-
sound speakers and a mega-whopper
10-foot super-sized screen!

'You know, Mum, we wouldn't have
any arguments if we all had our *own*
TVs,' said Henry. Yes! In fact, if he had
two in his bedroom, and a third one
spare in case one of
them ever broke, he'd
never argue about
the telly again.

Mum sighed. 'Just
find the remote,'
she said. 'It
must be here
somewhere.'

20

'But our TV is so old,' said Henry.

'It's fine,' said Dad.

'It's horrible,' said Henry.

'We'll see,' said Mum.

New TV here I come, thought Horrid Henry happily.

Mum sat down on the sofa and opened her book.

Dad sat down on the sofa and opened his book.

Peter sat down on the sofa and opened his book.

'You know,' said Mum, 'it's lovely and peaceful without the telly.'

'Yes,' said Dad.

'No squabbling,' said Mum.

'No screaming,' said Dad.

'Loads of time to read good books,' said Mum.

They smiled at each other.

'I think we should be a telly-free home from now on,' said Dad.

'Me too,' said Mum.

'That's a great idea,' said Perfect Peter. 'More time to do homework.'

'What??'' screamed Horrid Henry. He thought his heart would stop. No TV? No TV? 'NOOOOOOOOOOOO! NOOOOOOOOOOO! NOOOOOOOOOOO!'

BANG! ZAP! KER-POW!

'Go mutants!' yelped Horrid Henry, bouncing up and down in the comfy black chair.

Mum and Dad had resisted buying a new telly for two long hard horrible weeks. Finally they'd given in. Of course they hadn't bought a big mega-whopper super-duper telly. Oh no. They'd bought the teeniest, tiniest, titchiest telly they could.

Still. It was a *bit* bigger than the old one. And the remote could always go missing again . . .

# 2

# HORRID HENRY'S SCHOOL ELECTION

Yack yack yack yack yack.

Horrid Henry's legs ached. His head ached. His bottom really ached. How much longer would he have to sit on this hard wooden floor and listen to Mrs Oddbod witter on about hanging up coats and no running in the corridors and walking down staircases on the right-hand side? Why were school assemblies so boring? If he were head, assemblies would be about the best TV programmes, competitions for gruesome

25

grub recipes and speed-eating contests.

Yack. Yack. Yack. Yack. Yack.

Zoom . . . Zoom . . . Squawk! Horrid Henry's hawk swooped and scooped up Mrs Oddbod in his fearsome beak.

Chomp.

Chomp.

Ch– Wait a minute. What was she saying?

'School elections will be held next week,' said Mrs Oddbod. 'For the first time ever you'll be electing a School Council President. Now I want

26

everyone to think of someone they believe would make an outstanding President. Someone who will make important decisions which will affect everyone, someone worthy of this high office, someone who will represent this school . . .'

Horrid Henry snorted. School elections? Phooey! Who'd want to be School Council President? All that responsibility . . . all that power . . . all that glory . . . Wait. What was he thinking? Who *wouldn't* want to be?

Imagine, being President! He'd be king, emperor, Lord High Master of the Universe! He'd make Mrs Oddbod walk the plank. He'd send Miss Battle-Axe to be a galley slave. He'd make playtime last for five hours. He'd ban all salad and vegetables from school dinners and just serve sweets! And Fizzywizz drinks! And

27

everyone would have to bow down to
him as they entered the school! And
give him chocolate every day.

President Henry. His Honour,
President Henry. It had a nice ring. So
did King Henry. Emperor Henry would
be even better though. He'd change his
title as soon as he got the
throne.

And all he had to
do was win the
election.

Shout!

Shriek!

'Silence!'

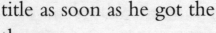

screeched Mrs Oddbod. 'Any more
noise and playtime will be cancelled!'

Huumph, that was one thing that
would never happen when he was
School President. In fact, he'd make it a
rule that anyone who put their hand up

in class would get sent to him for punishment. There'd only be shouting out in *his* school.

'Put up your hand if you wish to nominate someone,' said Mrs Oddbod.

Sour Susan's hand shot up. 'I nominate Margaret,' she said.

'I accept!' yelled Margaret, preening.

Horrid Henry choked. Margaret? Bossyboots Margaret *President*? She'd be a disaster, a horrible, grumpy, grouchy, moody disaster. Henry would never hear the end of it. Her head would swell so much it would burst. She'd be swaggering all over the place, ordering everyone around, boasting, bossing, showing off . . .

Horrid Henry's hand shot up. 'I nominate . . . me!' he shrieked.

'You?' said Mrs Oddbod coldly.

'Me,' said Horrid Henry.

'I second it,' shouted Rude Ralph.

Henry beamed at Ralph. He'd make Ralph his Grand Vizier. Or maybe Lord High Executioner.

'Any more nominations?' said Mrs Oddbod. She looked unhappy. 'Come on, Bert, what would you do to improve the school?'

'I dunno,' said Bert.

'Clare?' said Mrs Oddbod.

'More fractions!' said Clare.

Horrid Henry caught Ralph's eye.

'Boo!' yelled Ralph. 'Down with Clare!'

'Yeah, boo!' yelled Dizzy Dave.

'Boo!' hissed Horrid Henry.

'Last chance to nominate anyone else,' said Mrs Oddbod desperately.

Silence.

'All right,' said Mrs Oddbod, 'you have two candidates for President. Posters can be displayed from tomorrow. Speeches the day after tomorrow. Good luck to both candidates.'

Horrid Henry glared at Moody Margaret.

Moody Margaret glared at Horrid Henry.

31

I'll beat that grumpface frog if it's the last thing I do, thought Horrid Henry.

I'll beat that pongy pants pimple if it's the last thing I do, thought Moody Margaret.

'Vote Margaret! Margaret for President!' trilled Sour Susan the next day, as she and Margaret handed out leaflets during playtime.

'Ha ha Henry, I'm going to win, and you're not!' chanted Margaret, sticking out her tongue.

'Yeah Henry, Margaret's going to win,' said Sour Susan.

'Oh yeah?' said Henry. Wait till she saw his fantastic campaign posters with the big picture of King Henry the Horrible.

'Yeah.'

'We'll see about that,' said Horrid Henry.

He'd better start
campaigning at once.
Now, whose votes could
he count on?

Ralph's for sure. And,
uh ... um ... uhmmmm
... Ralph.

Toby *might* vote for
him but he'd probably have to
beg. Hmmm. Two votes were not
enough to win. He'd have to get more
support. Well, no time like the present
to remind everyone what a great guy he
was.

Zippy Zoe zipped past. Horrid Henry
smiled at her. Zoe stopped dead.

'Why are you smiling at me, Henry?'
said Zippy Zoe. She checked to see if
she'd come to school wearing pyjamas
or if her jumper had a big hole.

'Just because it's so nice to see you,'

said Horrid Henry. 'Will you
vote for me for President?'

Zoe stared at him.
'Margaret gave me a pencil
with her name on it,' said
Zoe. 'And a sticker. What
will *you* give me?'

Give? Give? Horrid Henry liked
getting. He did not like giving. So
Margaret was bribing people, was she?
Well, two could play at that game. He'd
bring loads of sweets into school
tomorrow and hand them out to
everyone who promised to vote for
him. That would guarantee victory!
And he'd make sure that everyone had
to give *him* sweets after he'd won.

Anxious Andrew walked by wearing a
'Margaret for President' sticker.

'Oooh, Andrew, I wouldn't vote for
her,' said Henry. 'Do you know what

she's planning to do?' Henry whispered in Andrew's ear. Andrew gasped.

'No,' said Andrew.

'Yes,' said Henry. 'And ban crisps, too. You know what an old bossyboots Margaret is.'

Henry handed him a leaflet.

Andrew looked uncertain.

'Vote for me and I'll make you Vice-Chairman of the Presidential Snacks Sub-committee.'

'Oooh,' said Andrew.

Henry promised the same job to Dizzy Dave, Jolly Josh, and Weepy William.

He promised Needy Neil his mum could sit with him in class. He promised Singing Soraya she could sing every day in assembly. He promised Greedy Graham there'd be ice cream every day for lunch.

The election is in the bag, thought Horrid Henry gleefully. He fingered the magic marker in his pocket. Tee hee. Just wait till Margaret saw how he was planning to graffiti her poster! And wasn't it lucky it was impossible to graffiti *his* name or change it to something rude. Shame, thought Horrid Henry, that Peter wasn't running for President. If you crossed out the 't' and the 'r' you'd get 'Vote for Pee'.

VOTE FOR PETER

Horrid Henry strolled over to the wall where the campaign posters were displayed.

Huh?

What?

A terrible sight met his eyes. His 'Vote for Henry' posters had been defaced. Instead of his crowned head, a horrible picture of a chicken's head had been glued on top of his body. And the 'ry' of his name had been crossed out.

Beneath it was written:

**Cluck cluck yuck!** Vote for a Hen? No way!

What a dirty trick, thought Horrid Henry indignantly.

37

How dare Margaret deface his posters! Just because he'd handed out leaflets showing Margaret with a frog's face. Margaret *was* a frog-face. The school needed to know the truth about her.

Well, no more Mr Nice Guy. This was war.

Moody Margaret entered the

Be on Target
Vote Margaret

playground. A terrible sight met her eyes. All her 'Vote Margaret' posters had been defaced. Huge beards and moustaches had been drawn on every one. Beneath the picture, instead of 'Be on target! Vote Margaret!' the words now read:

The next poster read:

How dare Henry graffiti over her posters! I'll get you Henry, thought Margaret. Just wait until tomorrow.

The next day was campaign speech day. Horrid Henry sat on the stage with Moody Margaret in front of the entire school. He was armed and ready. Margaret would be blasted from the race. As Margaret rose to speak, Henry made a horrible, gagging face.

'We face a great danger,' said Moody Margaret. 'Do you want a leader like me? Or a loser like Henry? Do you want someone who will make you proud of this school? Or someone like Henry who will make you ashamed? *I* will be the best President ever. I'm already Captain of the Football Team. I know how to tell people what to do. This school will be heaven with me in charge. Remember, a vote for me will brighten every school day.'

'Go Margaret!' yelled Sour Susan as Margaret sat down.

Horrid Henry rose to speak.

'When I'm President,' said Horrid Henry, 'I promise a Goo-Shooter day! I promise a Gross-Out day! With my best friend Marvin the Maniac presenting the prize. School will start at lunchtime, and end after playtime. Gobble and Go will run the school cafeteria. I promise no homework! I promise skateboarding in the hall! I promise ice cream! And sweets!

'If you vote for Margaret, you'll get a dictator. And how do I know this? Because I have discovered her top-secret plans!' Horrid Henry pulled out a piece of paper covered in writing and showed it to the hall. 'Just listen to what she wrote:

Margaret's Top Secret
Plans for when I am President

The school day is too short. School
will end at 6.00 when I'm in charge

I look at my school lunch and I think,
'Why is there a desert on my plate when
there should be more vegetables?'
All sweets and desserts will be banned

'I never wrote that!' screeched
Margaret.

'She would say that, wouldn't she?'
said Henry smoothly. 'But the voters
need to know the truth.'

'He's lying!' shouted Margaret.

'Don't be fooled, everyone! Margaret
will ban sweets! Margaret will ban

crisps! Margaret will make you do lots
more homework. Margaret wants to
have school seven days a week.

There isn't enough homework at this
School. Five hours of homework
every night

Get rid of school holidays. Who needs
them?

Ban chips!

Ban football!

Ban playtime!

'So vote Henry if you want to stop
this evil fiend! Vote Henry for loads of
sweets! Vote Henry for loads of fun! Vote
Henry for President!'

'Henry! Henry! Henry!' shouted Ralph,
as Henry sat down to rapturous applause.

He'd done it! He'd won! And by a
landslide. Yes!! He was President Lord
High Master of the Universe! Just wait
till he started bossing everyone around!
Margaret had been defeated – at last!

Mrs Oddbod glared at Henry as they
sat in her office after the results had
been announced. She looked grey.
'As President, you will call the school
council meeting to order. You will
organise the toilet tidy rota. You will
lead the litter collection every playtime.'

Horrid Henry's knees felt weak.

Toilet . . . tidy . . . rota? Litter? What??
*That* was his job? That's why he'd schemed
and bribed and fought and campaigned
and given away all those sweets?

Where was his throne? His title? His
power?

NOOO!

'I resign!' said Horrid Henry.

# 3

# HORRID HENRY'S BAD PRESENT

Ding dong.

'I'll get it!' shrieked Horrid Henry. He jumped off the sofa, pushed past Peter, ran to the door, and flung it open.

'Hi, Grandma,' said Horrid Henry. He looked at her hopefully. Yes! She was holding a huge carrier bag. Something lumpy and bumpy bulged inside. But not just any old something, like knitting or a spare jumper. Something big. Something ginormous. That meant ... that meant ... yippee!

Horrid Henry loved it when Grandma visited, because she often brought him a present. Mum and Dad gave really boring presents, like socks and dictionaries and games like Virtual Classroom and Name that Vegetable.

Grandma gave really great presents, like fire engines with wailing sirens, shrieking zombies with flashing lights, and once, even the Snappy Zappy Critters that Mum and Dad had said he couldn't have even if he begged for a million years.

'Where's my present?' said Horrid
Henry, lunging for Grandma's bag.
'Gimme my present!'

'Don't be horrid, Henry,' said Mum,
grabbing him and holding him back.

'I'm not being horrid, I just want my
present,' said Henry, scowling. Why
should he wait a second longer when it
was obvious Grandma had some
fantastic gift for him?

'Hi, Grandma,' said Peter. 'You know
you don't need to bring *me* a present
when you come to visit. You're the
present.'

Horrid Henry's foot longed to kick
Peter into the next room.

'Wait till *after* you get your present,'
hissed his head.

'Good thinking,' said his foot.

'Thank you, Peter,' said Grandma.
'Now, have you been good boys?'

'I've been perfect,' said Peter. 'But Henry's been horrid.'

'Have not,' said Henry.

'Have too,' said Peter. 'Henry took all my crayons and melted them on the radiator.'

'That was an accident,' said Henry. 'How was I supposed to know they would melt? And next time get out of the hammock when you're told.'

'But it was my turn,' said Peter.

'Wasn't, you wormy worm toad–'

'Was too.'

'Right,' said Grandma. She reached into the bag and pulled out two gigantic dinosaurs. One Tyrannosaurus Rex was purple, the other was green.

'RAAAAAAAA,' roared one dinosaur, rearing and bucking and stretching out his blood-red claws.

'FEED ME!' bellowed the other,

shaking his head and gnashing his teeth.

Horrid Henry's heart stopped. His jaw
dropped. His mouth opened to speak,
but no sound came out.

Two Tyrannosaur Dinosaur Roars! Only
the greatest toy ever in the history of the
universe! Everyone wanted one. How had
Grandma found them? They'd been sold
out for weeks. Moody Margaret would
die of jealousy when she saw Henry's T-
Rex and heard it roaring and bellowing
and stomping around the garden.

'Wow,' said Horrid Henry.

'Wow,' said Perfect Peter.

Grandma smiled. 'Who wants the purple one, and who wants the green one?'

That was a thought. Which one should he choose? Which T-Rex was the best?

Horrid Henry looked at the purple dinosaur.

Hmmm, thought Henry, I do love the colour purple.

Perfect Peter looked at the purple dinosaur.

52

Hmmm, thought Peter, those claws are a bit scary.

Horrid Henry looked at the green dinosaur.

Oooh, thought Henry. I like those red eyes.

Perfect Peter looked at the green dinosaur.

Oooh, thought Peter, those eyes are awfully red.

Horrid Henry sneaked a peek at Peter to see which dinosaur *he* wanted.

Perfect Peter sneaked a peek at Henry to see which dinosaur *he* wanted.

Then they pounced.

'I want the purple one,' said Henry, snatching it out of Grandma's hand. 'Purple rules.'

'*I* want the purple one,' said Peter.

'I said it first,' said Henry. He clutched the Tyrannosaurus tightly. How could he have hesitated for a moment? What was he thinking? The purple one was best. The green one was horrible. Who ever heard of a green T-Rex anyway?

Perfect Peter didn't know what to say. Henry *had* said it first. But the purple Tyrannosaurus was so obviously better than the green. Its teeth were pointier. Its scales were scalier. Its big clumpy feet were so much clumpier.

'I *thought* it first,' whimpered Peter.

Henry snorted. 'I thought it first, *and* I said it first. The purple one's mine,' he said. Just wait until he showed it to the

Purple Hand Gang. What a guard it would make.

Perfect Peter looked at the purple dinosaur.

Perfect Peter looked at the green dinosaur.

Couldn't he be perfect and accept the green one? The one Henry didn't want?

'But I'm obviously the best,' hissed the purple T-Rex. 'Who'd want the boring old green one? Blecccchhhh.'

'It's true, I'm not as good as the purple one,' sobbed the green dinosaur. 'The purple is for big boys, the green is for babies.'

'I want the purple one!' wailed Peter. He started to cry.

'But they're exactly the same,' said Mum. 'They're just different colours.'

'I want the purple one!' screamed Henry and Peter.

'Oh dear,' said Grandma.

'Henry, you're the eldest, let Peter have the purple one,' said Dad.

WHAT?

'NO!' said Horrid Henry. 'It's mine.' He clutched it tightly.

'He's only little,' said Mum.

'So?' said Horrid Henry. 'It's not fair. I want the purple one!'

'Give it to him, Henry,' said Dad.

'NOOOOOOO!' screamed Henry. 'NOOOOOO!'

'I'm counting, Henry,' said Mum. 'No TV tonight . . . no TV tomorrow . . . no TV . . .'

'NOOOO!' screamed Horrid Henry.
Then he hurled the purple dinosaur at
Peter.

Henry could hardly believe what had
just happened. Just because he was the
oldest, he had to take the bad present? It
was totally and utterly and completely
unfair.

'I want the purple one!'

'You know that "I want doesn't get",'
said Peter. 'Isn't that right, Mum?'

'It certainly is,' said Mum.

Horrid Henry pounced. He was a ginormous crocodile chomping on a very chewy child.

'AAAIIIEEEEE!' screamed Peter. 'Henry bit me.'

'Don't be horrid, Henry!' shouted Mum. 'Poor Peter.'

'Serves him right!' shrieked Horrid Henry. 'You're the meanest parents in the world and I hate you.'

'Go to your room!' shouted Dad.

'No pocket money for a week!' shouted Mum.

'Fine!' screamed Horrid Henry.

Horrid Henry sat in his bedroom.
He glared at the snot-green dinosaur
scowling at him from where he'd
thrown it on the floor and stomped on
it. He hated the colour green. He loved

the colour purple. The leader of the
Purple Hand Gang deserved the purple
Dinosaur Roar.

He'd make Peter swap dinosaurs if it
was the last thing he did. And if Peter
wouldn't swap, he'd be sorry he was
born. Henry would ... Henry could ...

And then suddenly Horrid Henry had a wonderful, wicked idea. Why had he never thought of this before?

Perfect Peter sat in his bedroom. He smiled at the purple dinosaur as it lurched roaring around the room.

'RRRRAAAAAAAAA! RAAAAAAAAA! FEED ME!' bellowed the dinosaur.

How lucky he was to have the purple dinosaur. Purple was much better than green. It was only fair that Peter got the purple dinosaur, and Henry got the yucky green one. After all, Peter was perfect and Henry was horrid. Peter deserved the purple one.

Suddenly Horrid Henry burst into his bedroom.

'Mum said to stay in your room,' squealed Peter, shoving the dinosaur

under his desk and standing guard in
front of it. Henry would have to drag
him away kicking and screaming before
he got his hands on Peter's T-Rex.

'So?' said Henry.

'I'm telling on you,' said Peter.

'Go ahead,' said Henry. 'I'm telling on
*you*, wibble pants.'

Tell on him? Tell what?

'There's nothing to tell,' said Perfect
Peter.

'Oh yes there is,' said Henry. 'I'm going to tell everyone what a mean horrid wormy toad you are, stealing the purple dinosaur when I said I wanted it first.'

Perfect Peter gasped. Horrid? Him?

'I didn't steal it,' said Peter. 'And I'm not horrid.'

'Are too.'

'Am not. I'm perfect.'

'No you're not. If you were *really* perfect, you wouldn't be so selfish,' said Henry.

'I'm not selfish,' whimpered Peter.

But *was* he being selfish keeping the purple dinosaur, when Henry wanted it so badly?

'Mum and Dad said I could have it,' said Peter weakly.

'That's 'cause they knew you'd just start crying,' said Henry. 'Actually, they're disappointed in you. I heard them.'

'What did they say?' gasped Peter.

'That you were a crybaby,' said Henry.

'I'm not a crybaby,' said Peter.

'Then why are you acting like one, crybaby?'

Could Henry be telling the truth? Mum and Dad . . . disappointed in him . . . thinking he was a baby? A selfish baby? A *horrid* selfish baby?

Oh no, thought Peter. Could Henry be right? *Was* he being horrid?

'Go on, Peter,' urged his angel. 'Give Henry the purple one. After all, they're exactly the same, just different colours.'

'Don't do it!' urged his devil. 'Why should you always be perfect? Be horrid for once.'

'Uhmm, uhmm,' said Peter.

'You know you want to do the right thing,' said Henry.

Peter did want to do the right thing.

'Okay, Henry,' said Peter. 'You can have the purple dinosaur. I'll have the green one.'

YES!!!

Slowly Perfect Peter crawled under his desk and picked up the purple dinosaur.

'Good boy, Peter,' said his angel.

'Idiot,' said his devil.

Slowly Peter held out the dinosaur to Henry. Henry grabbed it . . .

Wait. Was he crazy? Why should he swap with Henry? Henry was only trying to trick him . . .

'Give it back!' yelled Peter.

'No!' said Henry.

Peter tugged on the dinosaur's legs.

Henry tugged on the dinosaur's head.

'Gimme!'

'Gimme!'

Tug

Tug

Yank

Yank

Snaaaaap.

Riiiiiip.

Horrid

Henry looked

at the twisted

purple

dinosaur head

in his hands.

Perfect Peter looked at the broken
purple dinosaur claw in his hands.

'I want the green dinosaur!' shrieked
Henry and Peter.

# 4

# HORRID HENRY WAKES THE DEAD

'No, no, no, no, no!' shouted Miss Battle-Axe. 'Spitting is not a talent, Graham. Violet, you can't do the Can-Can as your talent. Ralph, burping to the beat is not a talent.'

She turned to Bert. 'What's your talent?'

'I dunno,' said Beefy Bert.

'And what about you, Steven?' said Miss Battle-Axe grimly.

'Caveman,' grunted Stone-Age Steven. 'Ugg!'

Horrid Henry had had enough.

'Me next!' shrieked Horrid Henry. 'I've got a great talent! Me next!'

'Me!' shrieked Moody Margaret.

'Me!' shrieked Rude Ralph.

'No one who shouts out will be performing *anything*,' said Miss Battle-Axe.

Next week was Horrid Henry's school talent show. But this wasn't an ordinary school talent show. Oh no. This year was different. This year, the famous TV presenter Sneering Simone was choosing the winner.

But best and most fantastic of all,
the prize was a chance to appear on
Simone's TV programme *Talent Tigers*.
And from there . . . well, there was no
end to the fame and fortune which
awaited the winner.

Horrid Henry had to win. He just
had to. A chance to be on TV! A chance
for his genius to be recognised, at last.

The only problem was, he had so
many talents it was impossible to pick
just one. He could eat crisps faster than
Greedy Graham. He could burp to the
theme tune of *Marvin the Maniac*.
He could stick out his tongue almost
as far as Moody Margaret.

But brilliant as these talents were,
perhaps they weren't *quite* special enough
to win. Hmmmm . . .

Wait, he had it.

He could perform his new rap, 'I have

an ugly brother, ick ick ick/ A smelly
toad brother, who makes me sick.' That
would be sure to get him on *Talent
Tigers*.

'Margaret!' barked Miss Battle-Axe,
'what's your talent?'

'Susan and I are doing a rap,' said
Moody Margaret.

What?

'*I'm* doing a rap,' howled Henry. How dare Margaret steal his idea!

'Only one person can do a rap,' said Miss Battle-Axe firmly.

'Unfair!' shrieked Horrid Henry.

'Be quiet, Henry,' said Miss Battle-Axe.

Moody Margaret stuck out her tongue at Horrid Henry. 'Nah nah ne nah nah.'

Horrid Henry stuck out his tongue at Moody Margaret. Aaaarrgh! It was so unfair.

'I'm doing a hundred push-ups,' said Aerobic Al.

'I'm playing the drums,' said Jazzy Jim.

'I want to do a rap!' howled Horrid Henry. 'Mine's much better than hers!'

'You have to do something else or not take part,' said Miss Battle-Axe, consulting her list.

Not take part? Was Miss Battle-Axe
out of her mind? Had all those years
working on a chain gang done her in?

Miss Battle-Axe stood in front of
Henry, baring her fangs. Her pen tapped
impatiently on her notebook.

'Last chance, Henry. List closes in ten
seconds . . .'

What to do, what to do?

'I'll do magic,' said Horrid Henry.

72

How hard could it be to do some magic? He wasn't a master of disguise and the fearless leader of the Purple Hand Gang for nothing. In fact, not only would he do magic, he would do the greatest magic trick the world had ever seen. No rabbits out of a hat. No flowers out of a cane. No sawing a girl in half – though if Margaret volunteered Henry would be very happy to oblige.

No! He, Henry, Il Stupendioso, the greatest magician ever, would . . . would . . . he would wake the dead.

73

Wow. That was much cooler than a rap. He could see it now. He would chant his magic spells and wave his magic wand, until slowly, slowly, slowly, out of the coffin the bony body would rise, sending the audience screaming out of the hall!

Yes! thought Horrid Henry, *Talent Tigers* here I come. All he needed was an assistant.

Unfortunately, no one in his class wanted to assist him.

'Are you crazy?' said Gorgeous Gurinder.

'I've got a much better talent than *that*. No way,' said Clever Clare.

'Wake the dead?' gasped Weepy William. 'Nooooo.'

Rats, thought Horrid Henry. For his spectacular trick to work, an assistant was essential. Henry hated working with other children, but sometimes it couldn't be helped. Was there anyone he knew who would do exactly as they were told? Someone who would obey his every order? Hmmm. Perhaps there was a certain someone who would even pay for the privilege of being in his show.

Perfect Peter was busy emptying the dishwasher without being asked.

'Peter,' said Henry sweetly, 'how much would you pay me if I let you be in my magic show?'

Perfect Peter couldn't believe his ears. Henry was asking him to be in his show. Peter had always wanted to be in a show. And now Henry was actually asking him after he'd said no a million times. It was a dream come true. He'd pay anything.

'I've got £6.27 in my piggy bank,' said Peter eagerly.

Horrid Henry pretended to think.

'Done!' said Horrid Henry. 'You can start by painting the coffin black.'

'Thank you, Henry,' said Peter humbly, handing over the money.

Tee hee, thought Horrid Henry, pocketing the loot.

Henry told Peter what he had to do. Peter's jaw dropped.

'And will my name be on the billboard so everyone will know I'm your assistant?' asked Peter.

'Of course,' said Horrid Henry.

*

76

The great day arrived at last. Henry had
practised and practised and practised.
His magic robes were ready. His magic
spells were ready. His coffin was ready.
His props were ready. Even his dead
body was as ready as it would ever be.
Victory was his!

Henry and Peter stood backstage and
peeked through the curtain as the
audience charged into the hall. The
school was buzzing. Parents pushed and
shoved to get the best seats. There was a
stir as Sneering
Simone swept
in, taking her
seat in the
front row.

'Would
you *please*
move?'
demanded

Margaret's mother, waving her camcorder. 'I can't see my little Maggie Muffin.'

'And I can't see Al with *your* big head in the way,' snapped Aerobic Al's dad, shoving his camera in front of Moody Margaret's mum.

'Parents, behave!' shouted Mrs Oddbod. 'What an exciting programme we have for you today! You will be amazed at all the talents in this school. First Clare will recite Pi, which as you all know is the ratio of the

circumference of a circle to the
diameter, to 31 significant figures!'

'3.14159 26535 89793 23846 26433
83279,' said Clever Clare.

Sneering Simone made a few notes.

'Boring,' shouted Horrid Henry.
'Boring!'

'Shhh,' hissed Miss Battle-Axe.

'Now, Gurinder, Linda, Fiona and Zoe
proudly present: the cushion dance!'

Gorgeous Gurinder, Lazy Linda, Fiery
Fiona and Zippy Zoe ran on stage and
placed a cushion in each corner. Then
they skipped to each pillow, pretended
to sew it, then hopped around with a
pillow each, singing:

'We're the stitching queens
dressed in sateen,
we're full of beans,
see us preen,
as we steal . . . the . . . scene!'

Sneering Simone looked surprised. Tee hee, thought Horrid Henry gleefully. If everyone's talents were as awful as that, he was a shoe-in for *Talent Tigers*.

'Lovely,' said Mrs Oddbod. 'Just lovely. And now we have William, who will play the flute.'

Weepy William put his mouth to the flute and blew. There was no sound.

William stopped and stared at his flute. The mouth hole appeared to have vanished.

Everyone was looking at him. What could he do?

'Toot toot toot,' trilled William, pretending to blow. 'Toot toot toot—waaaaaah!' wailed William, bursting into tears and running off stage.

'Never mind,' said Mrs Oddbod, 'anyone could put the mouthpiece on upside down. And now we have . . .' Mrs Oddbod glanced at her paper, 'a caveman Ugga Ugg dance.'

Stone-Age Steven and Beefy Bert stomped on stage wearing leopard-skin costumes and carrying clubs.

'UGGG!' grunted Stone-Age Steven. 'UGGG UGGG UGGG UGGG UGGG! Me cave man!'

STOMP CLUMPA CLUMP
STOMP CLUMPA CLUMP
stomped Stone-Age Steven.

STOMP CLUMPA CLUMP
STOMP CLUMPA CLUMP
stomped Beefy Bert.

'UGGA BUG UGGA BUG UGG
UGG UGG,' bellowed Steven, whacking
the floor with his club.

'Bert!' hissed Miss Battle-Axe. 'This
isn't your talent! What are you doing on
stage?'

'I dunno,' said Beefy Bert.

'Boo! Boooooo!' jeered Horrid Henry
from backstage as the Cavemen thudded
off.

Then Moody Margaret and Sour
Susan performed their rap:

'Mar-garet, ooh ooh oooh

Mar-garet, it's all true

Mar-garet, best of the best

Pick Margaret, and dump the rest.'

Rats, thought Horrid Henry, glaring.
My rap was so much better. What a
waste. And why was the audience
applauding?

'Booooo!' yelled Horrid Henry.
'Boooooo!'

'Another sound out of you and you
will not be performing,' snapped Miss
Battle-Axe.

'And now Soraya will be singing
"You broke my heart in 39 pieces",
accompanied by her mother on the
piano,' said Mrs Oddbod hastily.

'Sing out, Soraya!' hissed her mother,
pounding the piano and singing along.

'I'm singing as loud as I can,' yelled
Soraya.

83

BANG! BANG! BANG! BANG!
BANG! BANG! went the piano.

Then Jolly Josh began to saw 'Twinkle twinkle little star' on his double bass.

Sneering Simone held her ears.

'We're next,' said Horrid Henry, grabbing hold of his billboard and whipping off the cloth.

Perfect Peter stared at the billboard. It read:

**Il Stupendiogo, world's greatest magician played by Henry**

**Magic by Henry**
**Costumes by Henry**
**Props by Henry**
**Sound by Henry**
**Written by Henry**
**Directed by Henry**

'But Henry,' said Peter, 'where's my name?'

'Right here,' said Horrid Henry, pointing.

On the back, in tiny letters, was written:

**Assistant: Peter**

'But no one will see that,' said Peter.

Henry snorted.

'If I put your name on the *front* of the billboard, everyone would guess the trick,' said Henry.

'No they wouldn't,' said Peter.

Honestly, thought Horrid Henry, did

any magician ever have such a dreadful helper?

'I'm the star,' said Henry. 'You're lucky you're even in my show. Now shut up and get in the coffin.'

Perfect Peter was furious. That was just like Henry, to be so mean.

'Get in!' ordered Henry.

Peter put on his skeleton mask and climbed into the coffin. He was fuming.

Henry had said he'd put his name on the billboard, and then he'd written it on the back. No one would know he was the assistant. No one.

The lights dimmed. Spooky music began to play.

'Oooooooooohhhh,' moaned the ghostly sounds as Horrid Henry, wearing his special long black robes studded with stars and a special magician's hat, dragged his coffin through the curtains onto the stage.

'I am Il Stupendioso, the great and powerful magician!' intoned Henry. 'Now, Il Stupendioso will perform the greatest trick ever seen. Be prepared to marvel. Be prepared to be amazed. Be prepared not to believe your eyes. I, Il Stupendioso, will wake the dead!!'

'Ooohh,' gasped the audience.

Horrid Henry swept back and forth across the stage, waving his wand and mumbling.

'First I will say the secret words of magic. Beware! Beware! Do not try this at home. Do not try this in a graveyard. Do not – ' Henry's voice sank to a whisper – 'do not try this unless you're prepared for the dead . . . to walk!' Horrid Henry ended his sentence with a blood-curdling scream. The audience gasped.

Horrid Henry stood above the coffin and chanted:

'Abracadabra,
flummery flax,

88

voodoo hoodoo
mumbo crax.
Rise and shine, corpse of mine!'

Then Horrid Henry whacked the
coffin once with his wand.

Slowly Perfect Peter poked a skeleton
hand out of the coffin, then withdrew it.

'Ohhhh,' went
the audience.
Toddler Tom
began to wail.

Horrid Henry
repeated the spell.

'Abracadabra,
flummery flax,
voodoo hoodoo
mumbo crax.
Rise and shine, bony swine!'

Then Horrid Henry whacked the coffin twice with his wand.

This time Perfect Peter slowly raised the plastic skull with a few tufts of blond hair glued to it, then lowered it back down. Toddler Tom began to howl.

'And now, for the third and final time, I will say the magic spell, and before your eyes, the body will rise. Stand back . . .'

'Abracadabra,
flummery flax,
voodoo hoodoo
mumbo crax.
Rise and shine, here is the sign!'

And Horrid Henry whacked the coffin
three times with his wand.

The audience held its breath.

And held it.

And held it.

And held it.

'He's been dead a long time, maybe
his hearing isn't so good,' said Horrid
Henry. 'Rise and shine, here is the sign,'
shouted Henry, whacking the coffin
furiously.

Again, nothing happened.

'Rise and shine, brother of mine,' hissed Henry, kicking the coffin, 'or you'll be sorry you were born.'

I'm on strike, thought Perfect Peter. How dare Henry stick his name on the back of the billboard. And after all Peter's hard work!

Horrid Henry looked at the audience. The audience looked expectantly at Horrid Henry.

What could he do? Open the coffin and yank the body out? Yell, 'Ta da!' and run off stage? Do his famous elephant dance?

Horrid Henry took a deep breath.

'Now that's what I call *dead*,' said Horrid Henry.

'This was a difficult decision,' said Sneering Simone. Henry held his breath. He'd kill Peter later. Peter had finally risen from the coffin *after* Henry left the stage, then instead of slinking off, he'd actually said, 'Hello everyone! I'm alive!' and waved. Grrr. Well, Peter wouldn't have to pretend to be a corpse once Henry had finished with him.

'. . . a very difficult decision. But I've decided that the winner is . . .' Please not Margaret, please not Margaret, prayed Henry. Sneering Simone consulted her notes, 'The winner is the Il Stupendioso—'

'YES!!' screamed Horrid Henry, leaping to his feet. He'd done it! Fame at last! Henry Superstar was born! Yes yes yes!

Sneering Simone glared. 'As I was saying, the Il Stupendioso corpse. Great comic timing. Can someone tell me his name?'

Horrid Henry stopped dancing.

Huh?

What?

The *corpse*?

'Is that me?' said Peter. '*I* won?'

'NOOOOOOOOO!' shrieked Horrid Henry.

# HORRID HENRY BOOKS

*Horrid Henry*
*Horrid Henry and the Secret Club*
*Horrid Henry Tricks the Tooth Fairy*
*Horrid Henry's Nits*
*Horrid Henry Gets Rich Quick*
*Horrid Henry's Haunted House*
*Horrid Henry and the Mummy's Curse*
*Horrid Henry's Revenge*
*Horrid Henry and the Bogey Babysitter*
*Horrid Henry's Stinkbomb*
*Horrid Henry's Underpants*
*Horrid Henry Meets the Queen*
*Horrid Henry and the Mega-Mean Time Machine*
*Horrid Henry and the Football Fiend*
*Horrid Henry's Christmas Cracker*
*Horrid Henry and the Abominable Snowman*
*Horrid Henry Robs the Bank*
*Horrid Henry Wakes the Dead*
*Horrid Henry Rocks*
*Horrid Henry and the Zombie Vampire*
*Horrid Henry's Monster Movie*

## Colour books

*Horrid Henry's Big Bad Book*
*Horrid Henry's Wicked Ways*
*Horrid Henry's Evil Enemies*
*Horrid Henry Rules the World*
*Horrid Henry's House of Horrors*
*Horrid Henry's Dreadful Deeds*
*Horrid Henry Shows Who's Boss*

**Joke Books**

*Horrid Henry's Joke Book*

*Horrid Henry's Jolly Joke Book*

*Horrid Henry's Mighty Joke Book*

*Horrid Henry's Hilariously Horrid Joke Book*

*Horrid Henry's Purple Hand Gang Joke Book*

*Horrid Henry's All Time Favourite Joke Book*

**Horrid Henry** is also available on CD and as a digital download, all read by Miranda Richardson.

'A hoot from beginning to end . . .
As always, Miranda Richardson's delivery is perfection and the manic music is a delight.'
DAILY EXPRESS

'Long may this dreadful boy continue to terrorise all who know him. He's a nightmare, but so entertaining . . . Miranda Richardson's spirited reading is accompanied by a brilliant music soundtrack – they make a noisy and fun-filled duo.'
PARENTS' GUIDE

# HORRID HENRY

The first book about the adventures of Horrid
Henry, in which Henry tries (unbelievably) to
be good, goes to dance classes, makes 'Glop'
with Moody Margaret and goes on holiday.

'Henry is a truly
great character'
*Sunday Times*

# HORRID HENRY
## and the
## Secret Club

Horrid Henry gets an injection, torments
his little brother Perfect Peter, creates havoc at
his own birthday party, and plans sweet revenge
when Moody Margaret won't let him into
her Secret Club.

# HORRiD HENRY
## Tricks the Tooth Fairy

Horrid Henry returns – and this time he tries
to trick the Tooth Fairy, sends Moody Margaret
packing, makes teachers run screaming from
school . . . and single-handedly
wrecks a wedding.

# HORRID HENRY'S Nits

Scratch. Scratch. Scratch –
Horrid Henry has nits!

And he's on a mission to give them to
everyone else too. After that, he can turn
his attention to sabotaging his school trip,
ruining his parents' dinner party
and terrifying Perfect Peter
with a Fangmangler.

# HORRiD HENRY
## and the
## Mummy's Curse

Horrid Henry has a new hobby,
tries to avoid learning his spellings,
creates havoc at the swimming pool,
and convinces Peter to turn
Fluffy the cat into a mummy!

# HORRiD HENRY
## Gets Rich Quick

Horrid Henry makes sure he gets the presents he wants for Christmas, sabotages the school sports day, runs away from home, and thinks of a brilliant way to get rich quick.